# GULITH

The Return Of Lancelot Biggs

Nelson S. Bond

ISBN: 978-1-63652-299-9

# THE RETURN OF LANCELOT BIGGS

## NELSON S. BOND

I guess it was about 7:58 Solar Constant Time—yes, it was exactly that, because I'd just received a clearance O.Q. for 8:00 from the Sun City portmaster—when the portal of my radio turret opened and in waddled Cap Hanson, skipper of our void-mangling freighter, the *Saturn*.

The Old Man's optics were dancing like a nudist in a hailstorm, and he wore a grin on his lips that stretched from ear to there.

"Guess what, Sparks?" he chortled. "I got a s'prise for you! Guess who just came aboard?"

I said gloomily, "If it's anybody like that sourpuss encyclopedia-on-legs who came aboard at Luna, you can have my resignation right now, if not sooner. I've been hectored and bulldozed and criticised so much lately that I'm beginning to feel like one large apology with corpuscles."

I wasn't joking, either. You know me—Bert Donovan—the easy-goingest bug-pounder who ever loused up the ether with Morse code. I don't get mad often, and my nerves are as steady as a forger's fingers, but this newest addition to the *Saturn's* personnel had me on the verge of babbling baby-talk.

His name was Horatio Gilchrist, his rank was "Major" and his title was "efficiency expert." To summarize briefly: Major Horatio Gilchrist was a rank efficiency expert—and I *do* mean rank! He had pale, green, watery, squinting eyes and a nose like a gimlet. Said proboscis was always in everybody else's business. He snooped and sniffed and sidled about the *Saturn* like a pup in the Petrified Forest, and he had a habit of popping out where least expected, like a fat man in tights.

He was always making suggestions. He told me how to conserve juice by pre-heating the tubes before I transmitted. He advised Cap Hanson, who has been roving the spaceways, man and boy, for more than forty years, on astrogation practices. He quoted facts, figures and statistics at Dick Todd till our acting First Mate grew as haggard as a parson at a burleyque.

"I can't stand it, Sparks!" Todd moaned to me feebly after a session with Gilchrist. "He's driving me whacky with his confounded 'efficiency'! The hell of it is half the time he's right! There *are* ways to save time, money and materials while operating the *Saturn*. We all know that. But you can't run a spaceship like an adding-machine!"

But such complaints were as futile as a bathing-suit on Mars. Major Gilchrist ranked every officer on the *Saturn*, and his "suggestions" had to be obeyed—or else!

Cap Hanson said commiseratingly, "I know, Sparks. I hate his g—I mean, *I* don't like the gentleman much, either. But, listen! This is something swell! The guy who joined us at Sun City is none other than—"

But he never finished his sentence. At that moment, the chronometer tagged 8:00, the hypos whined, the stern-jets roared, and the *Saturn* lifted gravs from Venus as smoothly as hot butter sliding off a griddle. My eyes opened wide and my mouth dittoed. There was only one pilot in space whose touch on the controls was that deft, that gentle!

"*Biggs!*" I cried. "Good old Lancelot Biggs!"

---

I turned and banged hell-for-leather out of my room, down the ramp, and into the control cabin, with Hanson vainly trying to lumber along in the suction of my slipstream. As I had guessed, it was my old chum and erstwhile roommate, Lance Biggs, at the studs. Beside him stood the dark-haired beauty who had been Diane Hanson, and was now Mrs. L. Biggs.

I yelled, "Lance, you knobby old son-of-a-scarecrow! Where

did you come from? Where've you been? How did you two get aboard—"

Biggs—*Lieutenant* Biggs to you, upstart!—swiveled and grinned at me. Marriage might have worked wonders on the inner man, I wouldn't know about that, but it had not changed his exterior in any way, shape or form. He was still the old lean and lanky, gawky and gangling caricature of humanity I'd always known. Tow-headed and wistful of eye and blessed with a nervous, oversized Adam's-apple that bobbled up and down in his throat like an undigested billiard ball.

"Hello, Sparks," he said mildly. "We came aboard at Sun City. We've been honeymooning. But my leave is up, now, and I've reported back for duty."

I said, "And, man! am I ever glad to see you! We've been one hop-skip-and-jump from the loony-bin on this trip—and I don't mean could be! We can use somebody who has a few brains—"

Biggs looked puzzled.

"Why? What seems to be the trouble?"

"Pig-headed bureaucracy, that's what!" puffed Hanson irately. "Take it from me, son, the Major—"

Then suddenly his gaze, slipping past me, grew wary. His eyes veiled, and his arteries stopped hardening. Without a pause he continued in a milder tone:

"—major difficulty seems to be that we need brushin' up on the latest space practices. We're a bit rusty, you know. So the Corporation has assigned a very capable officer to—Why, there he is now! Come in, Major Gilchrist!"

And in slithered the efficiency expert, glaring like a teetotaller in a taproom. As usual, he had a nasty comment for everybody. To me he said, "Sparks, you left your battery on! A sheer waste of valuable current, sir—*waste*! Be kind enough to go aloft and attend to it instantly!" Then, to the Old Man, "And you, Captain— surely you know the Company rule against allowing women in the control cabins of space-craft?"

Biggs, having set the studs into lock-posts, slipped from the bucket-shaped pilot's chair and walked to his wife's side. No, he didn't exactly walk, either. Biggs' locomotion can scarcely be dignified by that term. It is a stiff-legged sort of galumph, like an ostrich on ice-skates. But his tone held a proper degree of uxorious dignity.

"The *lady*, Major," he said, "is my wife."

But the old freezeroo didn't chill Gilchrist at all. He just sniffed down his long, sharp nose at Biggs.

"And who," he demanded, "might *you* be?"

---

It was Cap Hanson who answered. The skipper's voice was warm with justifiable pride. "Permit me, Major. This is my son-in-law and First Officer, Lt. Lancelot Biggs. He just reported back for active duty. I'm sure you've heard of him. He invented the V-I unit and the uranium speech-trap—"[1]

"Oh!" said Gilchrist frigidly, and stared at my chum like a vegetarian at a hamburger. "So *you're* Biggs? This is too bad. I had just succeeded in training Lieutenant Todd to a point of efficiency. Now I suppose I must start over again and teach *you* how to manage a spaceship!"

Imagine it! That kind of crack to Mr. Biggs, one of the brainiest spacers who ever lifted gravs! Dick Todd was a good guy, but he wasn't Biggs' equal by ten decimals! I held my breath and waited for the explosion. Cap Hanson's mottled old cheeks began to glow like a neon sign, and Diane *whooshed* like an enraged Bunsen burner. But Biggs spoke up hurriedly.

"Yes, sir!" he said. "Very good, sir! I'll be most grateful for your instructions, sir!"

That was the kind of palaver Gilchrist liked. For a moment he looked half human as a tight little smile shuddered along his lips. He said, mollified, "That's very sensible of you, Lieutenant. We may get along, after all. For a while I feared your—er—lucky accomplishments in the past might—er—make you a bit difficult. Have you plotted our homeward course?"

"Yes, sir," replied Mr. Biggs. He lifted a sheet of paper from the chart-desk, handed it to the Major. Gilchrist studied it briefly, lifted his gimlet eyes.

"Not bad, Lieutenant. Not bad at all. A little old-fashioned, perhaps—"

That was more than I could stand. If Biggs wouldn't take his own part, I had to. I burst out, "But, Major, Biggs just graduated from the Academy two years ago! How could his astrogation be 'old-fashioned'? There's not a better plotter in space. Lance has yanked us out of more troubles—"

"*Sparks!*" That was Biggs, warning me with his voice and with his eyes. "Didn't the Major tell you to go turn off your batteries? You'd better run along."

"O.Q.," I snarled. "I'm on my way. Come up and see me in my turret some time, Lance—where the air is fresher!" And I beat it before Major Gilchrist caught his breath.

---

So there it was. A couple of hours later I was sitting in my cubby-hole, still fuming over how the Holy Bonds of Matrimony had changed a once vivid and daring spaceman into a vapid and scary yes-man, when there came a knock on the door.

"If you owe me money," I growled, "come in! If vice versa, there's nobody home but us amperes!"

The door eased open, and it was Biggs. His face was sober. He said, "Sparks, can I talk to you for a minute?"

"Why don't you ask Gilchrist?" I snorted. "He gives the orders around here."

He closed the door behind him, snapped the safety.

"It's about Gilchrist I wanted to talk—"

"Then do your talking," I advised him rudely, "somewhere else. If I never hear that skunk's name again, it will be too soon."

"Don't be hasty, Sparks. He's not a bad chap. Just a trifle headstrong, maybe—"

"Some people," I scorned, "like spiders. There's no accounting for tastes. Headstrong? You could use that skull of his to split granite. And *you*—" My indignation rose as I talked—"you're as bad as he is! Feeding him the good old soft-soap till it ran out of his ears!"

"It doesn't pay," said Biggs in that peculiar, soft, schoolmarm fashion he sometimes affects, "to antagonize folks you have to get along with. Whether we like it or not, Major Gilchrist has senior authority on this ship. But we can talk about that some other time, Sparks. This is what I wanted to show you—"

And he hauled a plot-chart from his pocket, gazed at me anxiously as I scanned it.

Well, you know how plot-charts are. Nothing but one solid mess of figures, figures, figures. Trajectory, flight-velocity, loft and acceleration computations—all that junk. They're about as easy to read as the shorthand scribblings of an illiterate Choctaw. I passed it back. I said:

"Looks O.Q. to me. Why the corrugated forehead?"

"Look again, Bert," demanded Biggs. "Look carefully at those trajectory co-ordinates. I may be wrong, and I don't want to influence your opinion by saying anything, but—"

This time I got it. The figures joined together and formed a picture in my mind, a picture that startled me worse than a surrealist drawing. I gasped:

"*Sol!*"

---

Biggs nodded.

"Mm-hmm. That's what I thought, too. The course he plotted skirts the Sun. Swings past it at a distance of only ten million miles!"

I'm a lot of things—but one of the things I am *not* is unresponsive to suggestion. I broke out in a hectic sweat and started for the door.

"Oh, no!" I yelped. "Maybe *he'd* like to play pussy-wants-a-corner with the prominences, but not *me*! The nearest I want to get to any corona is to smoke one! The guy's nuts! I'm going to tell him—"

But Biggs grabbed my arm.

"It's no use, Sparks. I've already told him."

"You—you have?"

"Yes. And he said—" Biggs' larynx performed some incredible involutions—"he said he knew perfectly well what he was doing."

"And so do I!" I howled. "He's plowing us smack-dab into Sol's gravitational clutch! Well, I don't want some! I have no ambition to become part of a sunspot!"

"No-o-o," said Biggs thoughtfully, "that's one thing we don't have to fear. Gilchrist's mathematics are O.Q. Our velocity will be great enough to overcome Sol's gravitation."

"But what are we going to do," I stormed, "about the heat? 6000° Centigrade ain't exactly what I consider a cool, refreshing climate!"

"That's the trouble. I told him we'd be boiled like beans in a pot if we passed that near Sol, but he pooh-poohed my warning. Said our refrigerating system would keep us cool and comfortable." Biggs shook his head helplessly. "I don't know what to do, Sparks. After all, his word *is* law."

I moaned. "And how long," I asked, "before we begin to french-fry in our own carcasses?"

"About five days, Sparks. Five or six days from the current—" He stopped suddenly. His pale eyes glowed. His larynx began leaping up and down like a Mexican jumping bean. "*Current!*" he repeated. "But of course! *That's it!*"

"'Scuse, please?" I demanded, puzzled.

But Biggs shook me off with an evasion.

"Not now, Sparks I can't tell you now. There's no sense in both of us getting in trouble. But I think I know a way to convince Major Gilchrist we must change our course."

---

So a couple of days skidded by, as days have a habit of doing. About the middle of the second day, Hanson came up to my turret looking as confused as a stork at the Old Maids' Home. He said, "Sparks, I been hearin' funny things—"

"Your digestion?" I asked. "Or have you been dosing your asthma with that 90-proof cough-medicine again? That'll make you hear things and *see* 'em too—"

"That's enough," interrupted the Old Man coldly, "of them kind o' comments! What I been hearin' is bad. They's a rumor floatin' around that we're on a dead trajectory for Sol due to Major Gilchrist's course plottin'."

"Oh, that?" I said. "Forget it, skipper. Mr. Biggs knows all about it. He's got ideas."

"Well," said the skipper, relieved, "in that case, I guess everything's O.Q." And he waddled happily away. Which gives you some idea who's the real Master Mind on the *Saturn*.

That very same night, Diane Biggs stopped me outside the Officers' Mess.

"Sparks, have you seen Lancelot anywhere? I haven't laid eyes on him all day, and I'm worried."

"You ought to know better than to fret wrinkles into your pretty brow over that one-man quiz program," I told her. "He's O.Q. Right now he's engaged in some mysterious project of his own devising. When last seen he was swiping generator supplies from the storeroom. Don't ask me why, because maybe I know the right answer, and I don't want to have to tell."

"He—he's not going to get in any trouble, is he?"

"Well, not exactly," I chuckled. "Though things *may* be a trifle hot for a while." For I had seen the stuff Biggs had snaggled from the supply room, and I had also watched him sneaking out through the airlock to the *Saturn's* hull. I had a pretty fair idea what was going to happen, but I figured it was his pigeon, and I didn't want to upset the Bostons.

So that was all till the next day. But the next day everything happened at once.

---

To begin with, when I tried to make my daily contact with the transmitting station on Luna I couldn't coax so much as a squeak out of my radio apparatus. It was as lifeless as a Venusian swamp-snake on Pluto. I sweated and swore and got under the banks to find the trouble, but everything seemed to be O.Q. Wiring, rheos, ampies, all were jake. But the radio wouldn't rade. It just hissed and spluttered and murmured as feebly as a college girl in a parked car. The trouble was, I finally discovered, it wasn't getting any juice. Nary a bit!

Meanwhile, Dick Todd audioed me from the bridge. He fumed, "Sparks, for Pete's sake tell Garrity to turn down the thermoes! It's getting hot up here!"

Which sentiment I could personally double in spades. Because it was getting hot in my turret, too. My shirt was a dishrag, and my forehead was leaking like a rented rowboat.

So I called Garrity, but the Chief Engineer spoke up before I could ease a word in edgewise.

"Is thot you, Sparrrks?" he bellowed angrily. "It's aboot time ye were gettin' in tooch wi' me! Whut the de'il's the motter oop therrre? Yon contrrrol-turrret is michty nigh stewin' us in oor oon grrravy! Turrn off the heat!"

Well, I'm not dumb. Not too dumb, anyway. Two plus two equals Lancelot Biggs. That's why, when Capt. Hanson and Diane wilted into my turret a few minutes later, looking like a brace of parboiled lobsters, I just grinned at them.

Hanson's eyes were haggard with despair. He wailed, "Sparks— this awful heat! You know what's causin' it? It's because we're gettin' too close to the Sun, that's what! You told me Lancelot had everything under control. Where is he?"

"If I'm not mistaken," I assured him, "he's entering now by the portcullis gate."

And I was right. Hatless, jacketless, soaked to the belt with perspiration but grinning triumphantly, entered Mr. Biggs. He mopped his forehead and said amiably, "'Lo, folks! Hot, isn't it?"

Diane ran to his side fearfully. She cried, "Lancelot, you must *do* something! Daddy says this heat means we—we're going to plunge into the Sun! You mustn't let—"

Biggs smiled serenely.

"Now, honey, don't get excited. We're in no danger. This isn't solar radiation. *I* caused this heat."

Well, that didn't surprise me. I had guessed it all along. But Diane and her papa stared at him wildly. "What?" croaked the skipper. "You done this, son? But—but why?"

"Why, simply because—" began Biggs. But he didn't finish his explanation. For there came a savage interruption from the doorway. And in an angry, spiteful voice:

"Continue, Mr. Biggs!" snarled Major Gilchrist. "*Do* continue, please! I am most eager to learn why you performed this abominable act of sabotage!"

---

I said, "Oh-oh!" and looked for a hole I could crawl into and drag in after me. Mr. Biggs' grin faded. "H-hello, Major!" he faltered weakly.

"*Mister* Biggs!" raged the efficiency expert. "May I ask *why* you wound a dozen coils of uninsulated wire about the *Saturn's* hull and connected the electrical helix so formed to the power generators? Don't deny it, sir! I've been outside and seen your handiwork!"

Biggs said faintly, "Why, I—I—er—"

"You needn't lie to me, Mr. Biggs! I understand too well. You deliberately established a hysteresis field around this ship in order to create a rise in temperature—was that it? You wished to make us believe the Sun's rays responsible for the heat—isn't that so?"

It's a long worm that has no turning. Biggs finally asserted himself. He raised his quiet but determined eyes to those of the Corporation official.

"Yes, sir!" he said. "That is exactly what I did."

"And why, sir?" demanded Gilchrist venomously.

"Because, sir, a close study of the course-chart has convinced me that we are in grave peril if we continue on our present trajectory."

"What! You question my astrogation, Lieutenant?"

"Excuse me, sir, but—I do!"

Major Gilchrist's gimlet beak quivered like a saucer of gelatin; his sallow cheeks flooded with color.

"Preposterous, young man! The *Saturn* will skirt Sol at a distance of twenty million miles!"

"The correct estimate, sir," disagreed Biggs gently, "is *ten*. I fear you neglected to take into consideration the space-warp created by Sol's tremendous mass. I have prepared alternative course instructions, sir. With your permiss—"

"Silence, Lieutenant!" Gilchrist was wild with fury now. He had no ears for logic. He wouldn't have listened to a first-run performance of Lincoln's Gettysburg Address, with sound effects by the original cast. "I've heard enough! You are guilty of having deliberately conspired to disturb, alarm and distress your shipmates, of having maliciously essayed an act of sabotage against your ship, and of flagrantly disobeying the commands of a senior officer.

"Your rocket, sir! You will go below instantly, and confine yourself to quarters under arrest!"

Lancelot Biggs said nothing. His larynx leaped, but without a word he stripped from his breast pocket that prized golden symbol for which all true spacemen would die, and with steady fingers surrendered it to Gilchrist. Diane stifled an impetuous little cry. Cap Hanson, his beefy face a wreath of anxiety, said, "But, Major—"

"I advise you, Captain," rasped Gilchrist viciously, "against defending Mr. Biggs' piratical actions. One thing I will not tolerate is defiance of my orders.

"Donovan—" He turned to me—"you will remove the fruits of Mr. Biggs' labors from the *Saturn's* hull. The heat which now inconveniences us will vanish when we are no longer the core of an electro-magnet. But just to make sure that no further efforts are made to beguile us into terror created by non-existent dangers, henceforth *I* will assume responsibility for all electrical stores and equipment aboard. That is all! Get to work!"

Thus ended our gay little tea-party....

---

And of course it was just as Gilchrist had said. As soon as Biggs' fantastic maze of coils and wiring was removed from the *Saturn's* hull, the thermometer crept back to normal. But friend Fahrenheit wasn't the only low thing on the *Saturn* that evening. My spirits were *beaucoup* slumpy when I slipped around to visit Mr. Biggs after dinner.

He was pathetically glad to see me, but apprehensive on my account. "You—you won't get in any trouble, Sparks?"

I said, "You're under arrest, but the balloon-headed little slob didn't say anything about solitary confinement—probably because he didn't think of it. Lance, what the hell are we going to do? I just ran over our figures again, and I got gooseflesh looking at them. The *Saturn's* approaching the critical spot. If we don't do something—and damn soon—to make Gilchrist change his mind—"

"I've been thinking feverishly, Sparks. You know my motto: 'Get the theory first!' I thought that by heating the ship I might frighten Gilchrist into changing course. But he caught on to my little trick."

"And we can't try it again," I fumed, "because Major Nuisance has put all the electrical equipment under lock-and-key. In another twenty-four hours this freighter is going to be a bake-oven—"

"I know," mourned Biggs. "And Diane—" He stopped suddenly. "Eh? What was that? What did you say, Sparks?"

"Nothing," I told him glumly. "I was just moaning."

"Oven!" cried Biggs. "Bake-oven! Of course! Ovens aren't all electrical. Listen—you know where the main fuel valve lies?"

"Why—why, yes. But—"

"Then get down there—quick! And shove the release lever to *Emergency Discharge* position!"

"And—and dump all those good tons of crude oil off into space?" I gasped. "Lance, you've lost your mind!"

"Don't argue with me! Do what I say! Oh, something else—are you familiar with the refrigerating system?"

"I'd better be. We're going to need it soon—"

"Go to the condensation-valve and close it. Be sure it's tight, Sparks. Smash it if you have to!"

I stared at him stupidly. It didn't make sense, but then the brilliant plots of Lancelot Biggs seldom do. I said hopefully, "You—you think it'll work, Lance?"

"It has to!" he retorted grimly. "Or—but hurry!"

---

So I did what he told me. I moved the release lever of the fuel oil emergency discharge to wide open position. I shed a salty tear as I did it. It almost broke my economical heart to watch those tons upon tons of thick, black goo flood from their storage tanks out through the for'rd vent into the empty reaches of space.

Then I found the condensation-valve and jammed it as Biggs had directed. Then, not knowing what else to do, I sat down and waited.

I didn't have to wait long. Results began resulting immediately, if not more so. I suddenly discovered that once again—as earlier in the day—I was sweating. I removed my coat. That didn't help. I took off my shirt. No use. If I hadn't been dead certain that within a short time there would be visitors to my turret, I'd have jettisoned my southernmost garments, too. But having no desire to embarrass Mrs. Biggs, I stood fast. And stuck fast, too, by the way!

So things started happening. The Chief audioed from the engine-room. He hollered, "Sparrrks, thot domned heat is on again. Turrn it off; or bi-gawd, sirrr—"

Well, Biggs hadn't said anything about an allegiance with the crew, but it looked like a great opportunity to stir up a mild case of mutiny. So I said placidly, "Sorry, Chief, but I can't do anything about it. Take a gander through your *perilens*. You see that big red thing blazing out in front of us? That's what's causing the heat."

Garrity gasped. "Ye—ye mean the Sun, Donovan?"

"We're going to pass it," I told him, "at a distance of only ten million miles. Figure it out for yourself." And I hung up.

Then Doug Enderby called from the mess-hall. I gave him a dose of the same medicine. Then Harkness. He screamed like a stuck pig, and began demanding a change of trajectory. I told him, "Don't squawk to *me* about it; tell Gilchrist. He laid the course."

And I had just blanked the screen when in raced Gilchrist himself, followed by Cap Hanson, Diane, and Dick Todd.

"All right, Sparks!" bellowed the efficiency expert, "What are you up to *now*? I'll see that you get busted out of the service for this! Rank disobedience, conspiracy to break shipboard morale, plotting with an imprisoned officer, deliberate sabotage—"

Yeah—Biggs was right! Major Horatio Gilchrist was a nice guy, in a repulsive sort of way. I glared at him.

"Just a moment, Major!" I said boldly. "If you mean this heat, you'd better hunt yourself up another victim. You know perfectly well Lt. Biggs is in durance vile. And as for *my* having done anything, why—how could I? You assumed complete control of all electrical equipment."

Gilchrist raged, "But—but this *heat*! Somebody has made the ship unbearably hot again—"

"Some*body*?" I asked him shrewdly, "or some *thing*? I guess you've forgotten, Major, that our real peril—of which Mr. Biggs warned you—is our proximity to the Sun."

"Nonsense, sir! The Sun—"

"Is getting closer," I finished, "every minute. You have

undoubtedly looked at the ship's hull to make sure there are no wires or coils on it?"

Some of Major Gilchrist's cockiness had oozed out of him. He said uncertainly, "Y-yes, I did. The entire hull is thickly coated with some glutinous substance—"

---

Oh, golly! That was one thing which hadn't occurred to me. I had just sort of taken it for granted that the fuel I had dumped would have whipped away into space. Silly logic on my part, for I've run the spaceways long enough to realize that nothing ever floats away in the void; anything you chuck from a spacevessel shares your velocity and hangs right along by your side. But I made the finest dramatic act of my life; gasped, and clutched at my forehead wildly.

"The oil! Migod, the oil-tanks have burst! Captain Hanson, we're doomed!"

And the skipper, too, came through nobly. He moaned and raced to the wall thermo, whirled from it frantically.

"A hundred an' two!" he bleated, "an' gettin' hotter every minute! We'll be stewed like peas in a pot!"

Gilchrist's lips turned a sickly bistre. He ran his tongue over them and faltered, "But my computations—"

"Were wrong!" I told him. "Dead wrong! Take a look at these other figures. Lancelot Biggs' figures!"

And as I thrust the sheet of paper into his fingers, I reached out and elbowed the audio button that establishes a complete circuit of every chamber aboard ship. Instantly the babel of angry, frightened, complaining voices burst upon our ears. The cries of hot and terrified men demanding help from the bridge.

"—can't stand it a moment longer," came the cry of Enderby. "Change course, Skipper!" And from the engine-room the roaring blast of Chief Garrity: "Ye've no richt t' drive us t' death like this, Captain. Change coorrse, sirrr, or by the saints, there'll be *moootiny*!"

And that did it! Major Gilchrist's nerve collapsed. His self-assurance slipped from him like a robe from a strip-teaser's torso, and all of a sudden he was no longer a tough, gimlet-eyed, hard-boiled efficiency expert, but a nervous and very frightened Earth-lubber caught in the grip of forces too strong for him.

"Into the Sun!" he babbled wildly. "The *Sun*? Oh, I mustn't die like this! Do something, somebody! Captain, you must change the course. Use the other set of co-ordinates. I was wrong—"

That was all I waited to hear. I shoved the new set of figures into Todd's hands, shoved him toward the door.

"Get going, Dick! There's no time to waste! We—"

But before I could even finish, there came an interruption that turned my spinal column to a slow trickle of icy water. The plates beneath my feet seemed to sag momentarily, then rise and hurl themselves forward. I slipped and fell to my hands and knees—and found it hard to rise again! A dull weight fastened itself upon me. Nor was I the only person so stricken. Diane had tumbled, too, and Cap Hanson was holding onto an upright stanchion for dear life. Gilchrist lay prone on his puss, his face a mask of terror. And the audio rasped with an ominous cry from the bridge.

"Captain Hanson! Captain Hanson, sir, come quickly! We've been caught by Sol's gravs!"

---

Well, it was about that time my heart began pounding the hell out of my shoelaces. Up to now I had been disgusted and sore and fretful, but not in the least worried. In spite of Gilchrist's pork-patedness, I had felt a serene confidence that before danger actually threatened Lance Biggs would find some way to wangle us out of our difficulties. But now—

But now we were in a sorry mess indeed! Caught in a gravitational grip thousands of times greater than Jupiter's; a million times more deadly. Once, from afar, I had been the unwilling but horror-fascinated witness of the fate of a ship gripped by Sol's terrific attraction. A dark mote struggling futilely against the brazen magnet that beckoned ... a moment's brief and hopeless essay to escape ... then a tiny, ochre flame glinting wanly....

Such a vision must have been flashing, also, through the mind of Major Gilchrist. For from his prostrate vantagepoint he loosed a howl of sheer panic.

"Oh, no!" he screamed. "Oh, no! No! No! No!"

How long that monotonous denial would have continued there is no way of guessing. But Cap Hanson, who despite all his faults has little use for a fool and *no* use for a coward, put an abrupt end to it. Straining against the pressure that half-immobilized us, he lurched to Gilchrist's side, bent and silenced the efficiency expert's wailing with a sense-rousing slap across the cheek.

"Stop that, you damn fool!" he roared. "The audio's open! Do you want to panic every man aboard this ship?" And as Gilchrist relapsed into whimpering silence, he swiveled to me heavily. "Sparks, there's only one chance. The velocity-intensifier. Tell Garrity—"

The velocity-intensifier, or V-I unit to give it its more common name, was that device invented by Biggs which enables a spaceship to increase its normal cruising speed to an incredible 186,000 mps—the speed of light! I could see the Old Man's idea. Attain that velocity and we might break free of Sol's hold. I said, "Aye, sir!" and was just about to cry the necessary orders to the engine-room when:

"*No!*" The familiar voice of Lt. Lancelot Biggs rang through the turret. "No, Sparks! Don't do that! It is sure death! As our speed increases, so does our mass! We'll only accelerate our fall into the Sun!"

---

I remembered, then, that every cabin was hooked into a round-robin circuit, *via* telaudio. So though it would have been humanly impossible for Lancelot Biggs to come up to this turret now, he was as truly with us as if he stood beside us. I cried back answer.

"But what *can* we do, Mr. Biggs?"

And—most stunning surprise of all!—my words were echoed by the groveling goon on the floor! Major Gilchrist, his voice cracked and fearful, bleated, "What can we do? You must help me, Mr. Biggs! Save me—"

---

**Biggs was yelling into the speaker while Gilchrist babbled in terror.**

---

Maybe I was mistaken, but I thought I could detect a ghost of a chuckle in my gawky pal's voice. He said, "Major, according to Space Practice Law No. 3, section *viii*, 'A space officer convicted of malfeasance, or confined under suspicion thereof pending trial and conviction, may not offer, suggest, or cause to be given any orders, commands or directions which may affect his ship's course or trajectory—'"

"You're free, Mr. Biggs!" screamed Gilchrist. "Free to come and go as you please! I was wrong! You're not under arrest any longer! But save me! Save me—"

This time Biggs *did* chuckle. I heard him do it. So did every man, mouse and mess-boy aboard the *Saturn*. And—

"Very well, Major," he said. "Thank you! Todd, set the ship on the new trajectory."

Todd said, "H-huh?"

Cap Hanson said, "W-what?"

And I croaked, "J-just ... like ... that ... Lance?"

Biggs' tone wobbled as if he were nodding his head.

"Sure. Just like that. Make the necessary stud adjustments, fire the rockets designated in my alternative plot-chart, and shift trajectory. That's all! And, oh, yes—you might send a couple of men outside, Skipper, with disrupters. Have them clear the hull of that caked fuel oil so it will be a little cooler in here.

"Honey—" He was talking to Diane now—"I'll meet you up there in a few minutes. Wait for me!"

Major Gilchrist's eyes looked like two poached eggs. As the full meaning of Biggs' words dawned upon him, he began roaring. But angrily. And loudly.

"A trick! A dirty, low, mean, contemptible trick by a renegade officer! Mr. Biggs! Mr. Biggs, sir, I am placing you under arrest again! Remain in your quarters, sir, or—"

But Todd had already sprung to his task, I had given the orders to Garrity's crew, and Cap Hanson handled this new threat. Again he hunched over Gilchrist's struggling-to-rise form, and his voice was a whiplash of scorn.

"I wouldn't, if I was you, Major!" he warned grimly. "You seem to've forgot that a minute ago forty-odd men aboard the *Saturn* heard you beggin' Lance Biggs to save your scrawny hide. One more crack outa you between now an' the day we hit Earth, an' this whole affair will be reported to the Company, so help me Hannah!"

"And in case you think we can't *prove* it," I assured him sweetly, "it might interest you to know that I plugged in the audio-recorder five minutes ago. We've got a nice little transcription of everything you've said since you entered the turret. Would you like to hear *that* played at the trial?"

---

So that, boys and girls, was all. Except for a tiny conclave some time later in Cap Hanson's quarters. Biggs was there, and Diane, and the skipper, and of course yours truly. We were asking, and receiving, a once-over-lightly on what to all of us save Lancelot Biggs was still a deep, dark mystery. The Old Man said:

"So we really wasn't never in no danger at all, son? We never was going to run afoul of the Sun?"

"Well, yes," said Biggs, "and no. We would not have fallen into the Sun. But we *were* in danger. Our trajectory, as plotted by Major Gilchrist, within a few short hours would have carried us to a spot where Sol's blazing heat might have crisped every soul aboard to a cinder.

"It was necessary to convince Gilchrist of our peril before it was too late to avert disaster. Heating the *Saturn* artificially seemed the best way to do this. I tried to make him think Sol was burning us up yesterday, but he got wise to my little scheme for heating the ship electrically."

"And you," I said, "got jugged. And he gathered all the electrical equipment into his own paws. But, nevertheless, you did turn the *Saturn* into a stew-kettle. How?"

Biggs grinned amiably.

"Why, you ought to know, Sparks. You helped me."

"A mule," I admitted, "helps a man plow a field, but it don't know how or why. Not that I'm a jackass, but—"

"It was very simple, really. You turned the release valve, allowing the fuel oil to discharge from its tanks onto the outer hull. The hull became coated with a thick layer of oil. Now, think hard! Oil in a vacuum, heated by an outside source—"

I got it. I groaned. That's the trouble with Lance Biggs' logic. Once you hear it explained, it always looks so easy!

I said, "A convection oven!"

"Why, yes! It's a heating principle invented by Dr. Abbot 'way back in the Twentieth Century. A large, curved reflector—in this case the hull of the *Saturn*—concentrates the Sun's rays on a layer of black oil. A container, highly evacuated, retains all the heat thus formed, raising the temperature of the 'oven' to almost any desired height." Biggs grinned. "Our problem was not the heating of the ship. That was a cinch. Our only hard job was convincing Gilchrist that we must change our course before we got *too* hot."

Cap Hanson nodded sagely.

"An' your 'space-oven' worked fine, son," he acknowledged. "But they's still one thing I don't understand. The pressure. This ship's equipped with artificial gravs an' all them things. But I distinctly *felt* the Sun's gravs grab hold of us. That's when I got the willies."

Biggs said modestly, "You can thank Sparks for that, too. He did it when he jammed the condensation valves. Made the moisture-content of the ship's atmosphere rise. The grav plates, being electrical by nature, short-circuited. Thus we were all subjected to an extreme 'gravitational attraction' which was the direct result of a capacity overload—but which under the odd circumstances every one naturally attributed to the Sun's proximity." He smiled faintly. "You might say it wasn't the heat—it was the humidity!"

Which sage—if time-worn—observation was the last comment our insanely sensible First Officer would offer on the case of Major Gilchrist *vs.* The-Rest-of-Us. And since the efficiency expert withdrew into his shell and stayed there for the rest of the trip, nothing more happened to disturb the peace and tranquillity of ye goode shippe *Saturn* that voyage.

So Biggs is back! A slightly older, slightly wiser, definitely more conventional Biggs, now that he's a married man with responsibilities. And after all the messes his crack-pot ideas have got us into in the past, I guess we all ought to be glad he *has* settled down.

But—I don't know. Married or not, Biggs is Biggs. And wherever his gangling frame intrudes itself, things have a way of happening. For instance, next month the *Saturn* is taking off for Uranus on a simple, ordinary cargo trip. On the face of it, it looks like smooth sailing. But Biggs is back on the bridge. And—

Well—anybody want to make any bets?

---

[1] For previous adventures of the Interplanetary Corporation's whackiest wisest young officer, see copies of *Fantastic Adventures* for 1939-40.—Ed.